Desert

desert lark

dwarf hedgehog

five-lined skink

viper

agama agama lizard

beisa oryx

kori bustard

gerbil

Swamp

marsh owl

didric cuckoo

herald snake

bohor reedbuck

marsh mongoose

little bittern

water lily frog

lesser swamp warbler

purple heron

Nile crocodile

soft-shelled turtle

sitatunga

We Hide, You Seek

by Jose Aruego and Ariane Dewey

Greenwillow Books, New York

For Juan

Published by Greenwillow Books, a Division of William Morrow & Company, Inc., 105 Madison Avenue, New York, N.Y. 10016
Design by Ava Weiss   Printed in the United States of America   2 3 4 5 6 7 8 9 10
Library of Congress Cataloging in Publication Data   Aruego, Jose. We hide, you seek.
Summary: The reader is invited to find animals hidden in their natural habitat.   [1. Hide-and-seek — Fiction.
2. Camouflage (Biology) — Fiction. 3. Animals — Habitations — Fiction] I. Dewey, Ariane, joint author.
II. Title. PZ7.A5227 We [E] 78-13638 ISBN 0-688-80201-X ISBN 0-688-84201-1 lib. bdg.

Let's play.
We hide
and you seek.

We'll play too.

Ready or not, here I come!

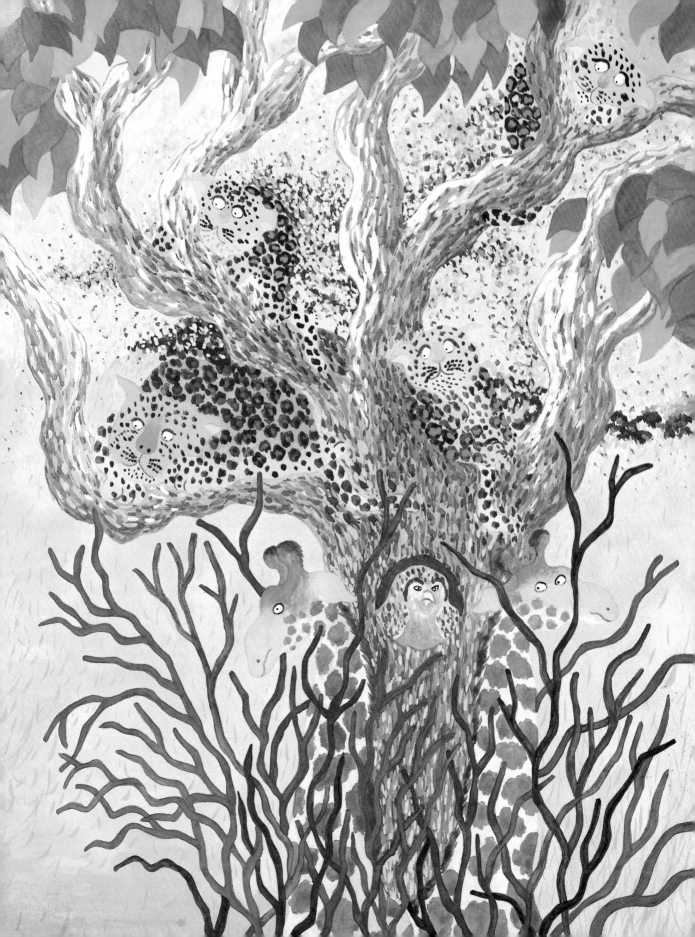

Now I want my turn to hide.

Where are you?

Plains

dusky nightjar

button quail

kongoni

silver-backed jackal

spotted hyena

zebra

scops owl

pectoral-patch cisticola

ostrich

cheetah

wildebeest

rosy-breasted longclaw

lion

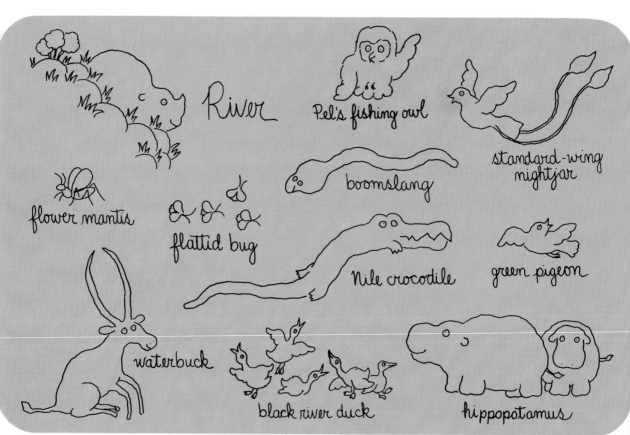

River

Pel's fishing owl

standard-wing nightjar

flower mantis

flattid bug

boomslang

Nile crocodile

green pigeon

waterbuck

black river duck

hippopotamus